MAX FLASH

MISSION 5

SUBZERO

For Janice and Steph

Darby Creek
A division of Lerner Publishing Group, Inc.
241 First Avenue North
Minneapolis, MN 55401 U.S.A.

Website address: www.lernerbooks.com

Library of Congress Cataloging-in-Publication Data

Zucker, Jonny.
Subzero / by Jonny Zucker ; illustrated by Ned Woodman.
    pages   cm. — (Max Flash ; mission 5)
Originally published in the United Kingdom by Stripes Publishing, 2009.
Summary: "Max Flash, amazing escapologist and master illusionist, returns for a cool fifth mission. Max is dispatched to the Antarctic to investigate a distress signal from a ship that has been trapped by a sheet of rapidly forming ice, and whose crew has mysteriously vanished. Could the crew's disappearance be connected to the sightings of strange beasts in the area? Max's investigations soon lead him to a secret base deep beneath the Antarctic ice . . . " — Provided by publisher.
    ISBN 978–1–4677–1212–5 (lib. bdg. : alk. paper)
    ISBN 978–1–4677–2055–7 (eBook)
[1. Antarctica—Fiction. 2. Monsters—Fiction. 3. Adventure and adventurers—Fiction.]
    I. Woodman, Ned, 1978– illustrator. II. Title.
    PZ7.Z77925Stp 2013
[Fic]—dc23   2012049478

Manufactured in the United States of America
1 — BP — 7/15/13

MISSION 5

SUBZERO

Jonny Zucker

Illustrated by
Ned Woodman

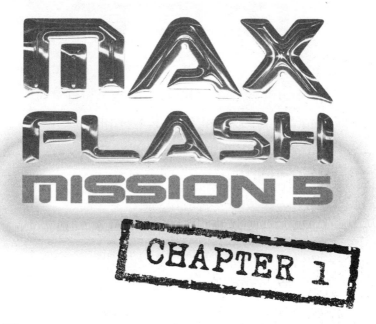

MISSION 5

CHAPTER 1

The wave was gigantic. It was at least ten
meters high. And it was hurtling furiously
towards him. Max was well out to sea. The
California shoreline was just a wavy scribble
of sand in the distance. He could hear the hiss
and roar of the water get louder as it smashed
onward.

Max took a deep breath as the wave sped
nearer. What he did in the next few seconds
was absolutely crucial. It didn't matter that he
was an excellent swimmer and could hold his

breath longer than most people on earth. If he timed things wrong, the crashing water would pound the life out of him. It would hurl him down, deep under the ocean's surface.

Max paddled forward with strong strokes. The swell of water picked him up. He leaped to his feet. He rode down the face of the wave, building up speed. Then the foaming crest curled over him.

From the shore Max couldn't be seen at all. Then the wave broke on the surface of the ocean. He flew out of the roaring tunnel of water. He was unhurt and utterly ecstatic.

"AWESOME!" he yelled, punching the air with delight.

Surfboarding champions of the world, watch out!

Max could just make out his parents on the beach in the distance. They were sunning themselves on loungers. He was about to swivel round on his board and go hunting for the next thunderous wave when he heard a metallic beep from his sunglasses. He pressed a tiny black button on the underside of the frames. A mini plasma screen slid down over the right lens.

The face of a woman with tightly scraped-back blonde hair and ice-cool blue eyes appeared on the screen. It was Zavonne. And she looked deadly serious.

MAX FLASH
MISSION 5

CHAPTER 2

Zavonne worked for the DFEA. (That's the Department for Extraordinary Activity.) The DFEA dealt with all matters that couldn't be trusted to the official authorities. Shadows are coming to life? Aliens from the planet Krystal 76 are entering Earth's atmosphere? The DFEA would get there first. They would "clean up." The authorities would never even realize something weird was happening.

Max's parents were stage magicians. They had carried out two missions for the DFEA. But

Max had now completed *four*. Zavonne had recruited Max because of his incredible abilities. He was a contortionist and escapologist. He was also a fine performer of illusions. He'd picked up his talent from watching and participating in his parents' stage shows. His DFEA missions so far had been intense. He had traveled inside a computer hard drive. He'd visited a distant galaxy. He had defeated evil sea creatures and taken on mummies brought back from the dead.

Zavonne's face made Max feel a mixture of disappointment and excitement. *Come on, Zavonne! I'm only on day three of my Californian Christmas holiday!* But then he began to wonder. *What kind of mission might it be this time?*

"Over the last couple of years a number of explorers have gone missing," said Zavonne. She didn't bother with a hello. "They all disappeared in a remote region of the Antarctic

known as the Bolt Zone. The Bolt Zone is named after Sir Travis Bolt. He is the explorer who discovered it."

Missing explorers in the Antarctic—cool, or should I say freezing!

"A group of international authorities are charged with overseeing this particularly inhospitable part of the world. This group believes the missing explorers died of hypothermia. Their bodies, however, have never been found."

"Buried under snow?" asked Max.

"That's one of the theories. The wind-driven blizzards out there can be vicious. However, over the years there have been several rumoured sightings of strange snow beasts in the region."

Snow beasts?

"What, like the Abominable Snowman?" said Max. He grinned.

Zavonne ignored his comment. "The DFEA

realizes these are only rumors. But the DFEA has always had an interest in the area."

Water lapped at Max's surfboard. He paddled the board away from an incoming wave.

"There are currently three scientists at the Bolt Zone Research Station. Dr. Savalle Klosh and Dr. Marion Holroyd are both very experienced. They are at the station for a five-year project monitoring climate change. Dr. Stella Jenkins is only there for a few months. She is on her own research project. Ten days ago, the three of them noticed something. The temperature in the area had dropped to an *unusually* cold level for this time of year. It's summer at present in the Antarctic. The days are very long. They have up to twenty hours of daylight. An average temperature for this season is about –8°C. But it had dropped to –30°C. This temperature is more usual for the winter months. The scientists predicted it would rise back to its normal parameters within twenty-four hours. But this did *not* happen. Instead the temperature has continued to fall. By last night it was registering –50°C."

"What do the scientists think is causing the drop in temperature?"

"They and the Antarctic authorities believe that extreme winds are responsible for this drop. They predict that matters *will* right themselves shortly. But even as we speak the temperature is continuing to fall. If the temperature keeps falling and reaches –100°C, there will be an ecodisaster on an scale never seen before. Ice will spread thousands of miles beyond its usual boundaries. The ice will affect water supplies and crops. This will have a huge effect on the rest of the world."

Max looked around at the clear water, amber sun, and aqua sky. The Antarctic was a very long way from his current sunny location.

"In fact," Zavonne went on, "the temperature drop has already had consequences."

"In what way?" asked Max.

"Two nights ago, a British navy vessel was on a training exercise in the region," replied Zavonne. "It was traveling less than three miles away from the Bolt Zone Research Station. It sent out a distress signal. I'd like you to take a look at it."

Zavonne's face disappeared from the screen. It was replaced by a fuzzy picture of a bearded man. He was wearing a navy blue jacket

adorned with medals. He looked extremely anxious.

"This is Captain Edward Hartnell of *The Triumphant*," he said gravely. "I am issuing a MAYDAY signal. In the last ten minutes, the ship has been surrounded by thick sheets of ice. It formed at a terrifying speed. We are unable to navigate in any direction. We are facing the threat of—"

Suddenly the screen went blank.

Zavonne's face reappeared. "There was no more contact with Captain Hartnell after that," she said. "The navy got a rescue helicopter out there as quickly as it could. They found no sign of any crew members. The navy has now dispatched an icebreaker to the scene. They will try to pry *The Triumphant* loose. They will tug it back to dock to examine it. They believe the ship's crew must have set out for the research station and perished on the way."

"But you don't agree?" asked Max.

Zavonne shook her head slowly. "We believe the extra-freezing conditions and the disappearance of the crew are linked in some sinister way," she replied. "And that, Max, is where you come in."

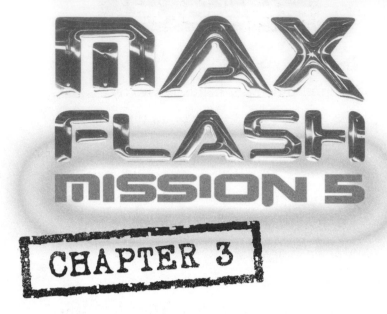

CHAPTER 3

Zavonne is sending me to the Antarctic!

"I want you to go out there immediately. You have three missions. Find out why the temperature is falling. Ensure that it doesn't reach –100°C. Find out what happened to *The Triumphant*'s crew."

So, no pressure then!

"You will be based at the research station. Your first job will be to get on board *The Triumphant*. Look for clues as to the crew's whereabouts before the icebreaker turns up."

"Er, small point," said Max. "How am I going to get into the station? I don't exactly look like a fully qualified climate change expert, do I?"

Zavonne pursed her lips. "Your cover story is that you are working on a student project about global warming. You will be reporting your findings back to an international student committee. Doctors Klosh and Holroyd would not be keen on having a child shadowing them. But Dr. Jenkins is fine about your visit. It goes without saying that she knows absolutely nothing about the DFEA or our activities. And it's vital that things stay that way."

"Is it just Jenkins, Klosh, and Holroyd at the research station?" asked Max.

"No," replied Zavonne. "A television survival expert called Gruff Addison is also stationed there. His cameraman, Jim Sweeney, is as well. They're filming his next series."

Gruff Addison! The *Gruff Addison!* The *coolest man in the history of TV? A man who*

can live for weeks in freezing snow caves, wade through ice lakes, and treat his own frostbite. The man is a legend!

Max was thrilled at the thought of meeting his hero. He wanted to question Zavonne further. But then he remembered something.

"What about my gadgets?"

"Return to your hotel room and await further instructions," Zavonne ordered.

Her face then disappeared from the screen.

CHAPTER 4

Max was back in his hotel room with his parents twenty minutes later. There was a knock on the door. Max hurried across the room and opened it. A man in motorbike gear stood on the threshold.

"Package for Max Flash?" he enquired. He held out a sparkling silver briefcase.

Max nodded and signed for the delivery. He closed the door quickly. He opened the briefcase. In one half was a stash of cold-weather gear. It had a small all-terrain backpack

and top-of-the-range snowsuit. Plus, it had extra-thick gloves, UV-filtering sunglasses, and a pair of high-spec snow goggles. Max's mom and dad watched as he pulled out each item and inspected it.

"Cool!" he beamed.

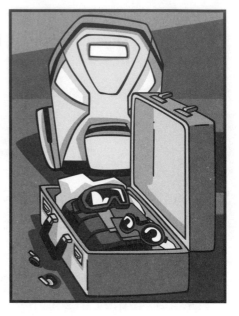

In the other half of the briefcase were three padded envelopes. One was blue. One was green. One was red.

"Open the blue one," instructed Zavonne's voice.

Max spun round. Zavonne's face was suddenly on the screen of his TV.

Is there anywhere she can't get to?

He opened the blue envelope. He pulled out a pair of tiny in-ear black headphones.

"Those are Ice-Cutter Headphones," explained Zavonne. "If you need to cut through ice, place the two ear pads against the surface about thirty centimeters apart. If you press on the earphones, they will cut out a circle of ice one meter in diameter. They work with ice up to a thickness of fifty centimeters."

Nice one, Zavonne!

"Now open the green one," she instructed.

Max fished inside the envelope. He pulled out what looked like a standard pack of mint chewing gum.

"That is a Gum-Shooter Stun Gun," said Zavonne. "When you rip off the top, three more packets will snap out to form a gun. The trigger is on the underside. This gun fires Crash Bullets. The bullets will stun opponents for ten seconds. It buys you time for your next move. You can use the gun for a maximum of twelve rounds. After that, it will become inoperable."

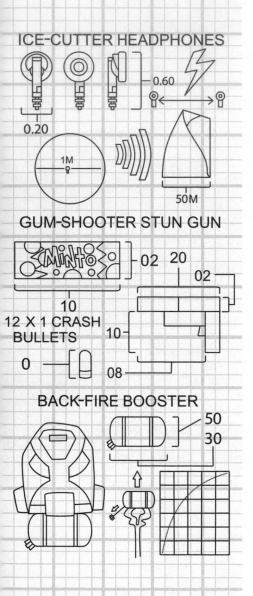

ICE-CUTTER HEADPHONES

0.60

0.20

1M

50M

GUM-SHOOTER STUN GUN

MINTO

02   20

02

10

12 X 1 CRASH BULLETS

10

0   08

BACK-FIRE BOOSTER

50

30

A gum gun! Excellent!

Max didn't wait to be asked before tearing open the red envelope. Inside was what looked like an extra-compact sleeping bag.

"That is a Back-Fire Booster," stated Zavonne. "The booster can be attached to your backpack like a normal sleeping bag. But it contains a powerful motor and fuel. Pull the white toggle. You will then be fired a hundred meters through the air. It will propel you at a maximum height of twenty meters."

Flying? Yes!

"But remember," said Zavonne.

"I know, I know," retorted Max. "The gadgets can only be used when I'm in extreme danger or facing death."

"In the backpack there's a map showing the positions of the research station and *The Triumphant*."

"So, when am I off?" asked Max.

"There's a small airport fifteen miles from your hotel," said Zavonne. "A plane is waiting for you there. This will take you to Chile. There you will switch to a helicopter. The helicopter will transport you to the Bolt Zone."

Max's dad went over to the dressing table. He grabbed the key to the rental car.

"The Antarctic is a dangerous and hostile territory at the best of times," warned Zavonne. "There's a strong possibility you will

be facing terrifying and unknown forces. And you will be working against the clock. I repeat that the temperature must NOT be allowed to reach −100°C."

Bring it on, thought Max. He examined his gadgets. When he looked up, the TV screen was blank and Zavonne had vanished.

"OK," promised Max, "I'll be extra careful."

His parents hugged him goodbye. Max hurried toward the plane. The DFEA pilot was a tall guy with a square jaw. He took Max's holdall and slung it into a storage unit. Ten minutes later the plane soared into the air. Max could see his parents waving from the ground. He took a deep breath.

Will I be coming back alive? Or will I freeze to death out there?

The flight to Chile went quickly. They touched down at another airport. A helicopter was waiting. Even though it was hot, Max changed into his snow gear. He'd need it soon.

The helicopter was incredibly noisy. Max had

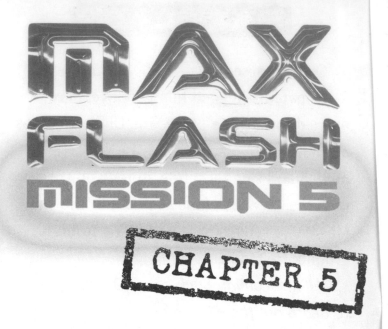

MAX FLASH MISSION 5

CHAPTER 5

"Be extra careful, Max," said his mom anxiously.
They were walking over the tarmac at the tiny
airport. The four-seater plane was just ahead.
Max was wearing his backpack. He was carrying
a holdall containing his snowsuit and cold-
weather gear.

"Look after yourself," said Dad. "It'll be
really, really cold out there."

"I thought it was going to be baking hot,"
quipped Max.

Dad gave him a look.

to wear ear protectors. He couldn't talk to the pilot or listen to music on his MP3 player. So he gazed out of the window. He watched as they flew first over the desert, then the ocean, and finally over huge ice sheets.

"That's the Bolt Zone Research Station," shouted the pilot. He pointed at three large, red, rectangular structures. They were interconnected by a series of transparent tunnels. They stood on a platform raised above the ground by giant steel pylons. Beneath the pylons at ground level was a large grey cube. It was connected to one of the red structures by a long ladder. On the roof of one of the buildings was a large dome. On top of

the others were three wind turbines and rows of solar panels.

"I can't land, so you'll have to use the ladder," the pilot shouted. He flicked a switch. A small panel on the side of the helicopter slid open. It let in a gust of fiercely cold air. The pilot pressed a button. A metal ladder shot out through the opening. The ladder dangled down toward the snow-covered ground. Max threw his holdall from the helicopter. He checked that his backpack was strapped on tightly.

"I'll take you as low as I can go," said the pilot. "Good luck."

Thirty seconds later, Max lowered himself over the edge of the helicopter. He started climbing down the ladder.

Everywhere around him was blindingly white. The ground, the mountains in the distance— everything. He saw a figure emerge from one of the red buildings. He reached the bottom rung. The figure headed down a walkway and hurried toward him. Max jumped down. His feet smacked onto the frozen ground. The ladder immediately shot back up into the helicopter, and it sped off.

"Dr. Stella Jenkins," said the figure. She smiled and reached out a ski-gloved hand to shake Max's. "Let's get you inside."

The scientist was much younger than Max had expected. She had large brown eyes and a small button nose. Strands of blonde hair pushed out from beneath her black snow hat.

Max picked up his holdall from the ground. Then he followed Jenkins up the walkway.

She tapped a code into a steel panel on the wall, and a door slid open. As they crossed the threshold, it slid shut behind them.

The first thing Max noticed was the cold. He'd expected it to be far warmer inside the station. But it didn't feel much different from outside.

"Isn't it a bit chilly in here?" he asked.

Jenkins nodded. "I'm sure you're aware of the rapidly lowering temperature situation," she replied. "Well, the station's heating system is also on the blink. Great timing, right! We keep fixing it. But it keeps on breaking down again. We can't seem to work it out."

Max studied his surroundings. He was in a large laboratory—the first red building. To his right was a workbench lined with microscopes and test tubes. Gleaming silver machines with black dials covered the wall on the far side of the room. To his left was a row of grey industrial thermometers with different

calibrations. Each gave a reading of –55°C.

The temperature is still falling—bad news!

In the middle of the lab was a long wooden table. Three computers and various notepads, journals, and digital printouts sat on the table.

"There's no Internet connection out here," said Jenkins. "But we do have satellite communications equipment." She pointed to a couple of large black machines. They looked like ultra-sleek DVD players with a slim, high-tech microphone attached.

At least we're not totally cut off from the rest of the human race!

Max spotted a huge mesh of unconnected, different-colored wires across the room. Jenkins followed his gaze. "Some equipment was stolen recently," she said.

"Out here?!" exclaimed Max.

"Yes, a few of our industrial thermometers. Weird, huh?" said Jenkins. "There's a research station further down the coast. But it's well over a hundred miles from here. And what would they want our equipment for?"

Jenkins took Max through a door on the far side of the lab. It led into a clear tunnel that led to the second structure. The first room had two sofas, three comfy chairs, a bookshelf crammed with scientific volumes, and a TV.

"The living room is where we relax," explained Jenkins. She lowered her voice. "Mind you, Klosh and Holroyd aren't exactly what you'd call the relaxing type."

Max laughed. Jenkins was all right. He followed her into a small kitchenette. It had a long, narrow table flanked by stools.

"The dining room," she announced. "The food here is just about bearable." She grinned. "But you need to be a fast eater!"

Before Max could ask what she meant by that, they'd moved on again. They went through another see-through passage. They were now in a hall with three doors on either side.

"The bedrooms," said Jenkins. "Small but comfortable."

She pushed open the furthest door on the right. "This one's yours."

There was just about enough space for a bed and a narrow wardrobe. In the corner was a small portable heater. "Dump your stuff and come and meet the docs," said Jenkins. "They're on the roof. We'll pop up for a quick hello."

Max dropped his holdall on the floor. Then he followed Jenkins up a metal ladder at the end of the corridor. They climbed through a trapdoor at the top. They stepped out on to the flat roof Max had seen from the helicopter. Crouching down beside a long line of tiny individual solar panels were two people. One was a portly man with a round face and a long moustache. The other was a thin woman with pale blue eyes and a short grey bob. They were deep in conversation.

"Dr. Klosh, Dr. Holroyd," said Jenkins. "This is Max. He is the young man I was telling you about. He's come out here to shadow me for that international student project."

The scientists looked up. Max gave them his most winning smile.

"Hello, Max," said Dr. Holroyd.

"Hello, Max," said Dr. Klosh.

"Doctors Klosh and Holroyd designed these new solar panels," explained Jenkins. "They provide a good power source. Especially in the summer, when we have twenty hours of daylight. And they're also excellent at melting ice very quickly. Which, as you can imagine, is extremely useful out here."

The scientists had already returned to their work.

Thanks for the big welcome!

"Don't worry about them," whispered Jenkins. "That's just their way. They're always like this."

Max would have liked to ask Klosh and Holroyd their thoughts about the radical temperature drop. After all, they were the experts. But he sensed that now might not be the right moment. Jenkins was already heading back inside. Max made sure the

scientists were still caught up in their discussion. Then he quickly bent down, picked up one of the solar panels, and dropped it into his backpack.

You never know when this might come in handy!

"Is Gruff Addison around?" he asked Jenkins hopefully. They were standing at the bottom of the metal ladder.

"Our great TV celeb," smiled Jenkins. "He's out on a shoot with Jim. Are you a fan of his?"

"Kind of," said Max. He tried to hide his disappointment.

They headed back to the laboratory. "Right, I've got to get back to work," said Jenkins. "I've got some interesting rock sediments to examine. You're welcome to watch."

"Er, if it's OK with you I'd like to get started on my project right away. You know, explore the local area," replied Max.

Starting with The Triumphant *to see if I can find any clues to the crew's disappearance.*

"Sure," said Jenkins. She reached over, grabbed a couple of small plastic containers, and handed them to Max.

"Collect a couple of snow samples while you're out there," she said. "We can look at them later."

Max tucked the containers into one of his snowsuit pockets. Jenkins slid open a large panel in one of the lab walls. It opened out onto a ladder that led to the grey cube. They climbed down. Max found himself in a large storage room crammed with equipment. He spotted four gleaming silver snowmobiles. There were also several pairs of skis, extreme-weather clothing, snowboards, and ice picks. He saw pretty much everything you'd need to explore a freezing wilderness.

Jenkins walked over to a rack. "What would you prefer," she asked, "skis or a snowboard?"

Max didn't think twice. "A snowboard," he replied.

He'd never been on a snowboard before. But he was pretty sure he'd be able to transfer his surfing skills. Jenkins handed him a sleek

blue snowboard. The she added a pair of extra-tough brown snow boots and a pair of lightweight snowshoes to fit over the top. "The snowboard snaps in two. That lets you store it in your backpack when you're climbing," explained Jenkins.

Ten minutes later, Max had positioned his snowboard on a ledge of snow next to the station. He checked his snowsuit pockets. He felt his gadgets nuzzling safely inside.

"Don't stray too far!" called Jenkins. She was climbing back up the ladder to the station.

"I won't!" cried Max.

He checked the map Zavonne had given him. He made sure he knew how to reach *The Triumphant*. Then he pulled down his goggles and launched himself down the slope.

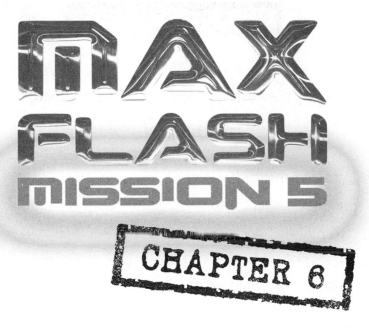

MAX FLASH MISSION 5

CHAPTER 6

Woohoo!

Max had been skiing a couple of times. But snowboarding was way more exciting. It was a bumpier journey than on skis. And it was totally exhilarating. He picked up speed quickly. He turned left and right, getting used to the feel of controlling the board.

This is wicked!

He sped past towering mountains threaded with hundreds of narrow crevices and enormous sheets of glistening ice.

This is like another planet. And I should know, because I've been on other planets!

He raced through a deep valley. A few minutes later he reached the base of a huge mountain. He snapped the snowboard in two and tucked it under his arm. He'd be needing it again soon.

Trekking to the summit of the mountain took about half an hour. When he got there he stood looking out over the edge. The vast expanse of ice below stretched as far as the eye could see. *The Triumphant* was about

a hundred meters from the shore. It was trapped in the ice's freezing grip.

Max fastened his feet onto his snowboard again. He flew down the other side of the mountain. He stopped when he reached the shoreline. He got off his snowboard and placed it in his backpack. He stashed the backpack next to a snow-covered boulder. He put on his snowshoes. The he stepped carefully onto the frozen ocean and slowly approached the huge ship. The nearer he got, the more he was amazed by the sheer size of the vessel.

There were small portholes at least twenty meters above him. They all looked tightly shut.

How inconsiderate to close all of the possible entry points!

He walked slowly around the edge of *The Triumphant.* Finally he spotted a porthole that was a tiny bit ajar. Max took off his snowshoes. He grabbed a jutting-out metal bolt. He pulled himself up, planting his snow boots against the side of the ship. Their superb grip held firm. He stretched out for another handhold. He pulled himself higher. A couple of minutes later, he was positioned right next to the porthole.

He pulled at the window to see if he could pry it open a little more. But it didn't budge. He tried this a few more times. On his fourth go he managed to create a small gap. He took a deep breath. Then Max began to squash his arms and shoulders into his body as tightly as he could. When his upper body was

compressed to half its usual width,
he pressed his head against
the porthole. He started
to squeeze his head
through the gap very
slowly. It was tight.
Max could feel the
metal rim digging into
his skull. His head finally
slipped through. And then
the rest of his body followed
quite smoothly.

*Now let's get on with finding some clues as
to the crew's whereabouts.*

Max took in the room as he straightened up.
It contained four bunks. *It must be the sailors'
quarters.* The cabin was incredibly neat. One
large trunk was stored under each bed. He
stepped out into a corridor and entered the
cabin next door. It was exactly the same as
the first.

He returned to the corridor. He headed for a large door at the far end. He stepped through. He climbed a flight of steps, which took him up and out on deck. It was a vast expanse. Wheels and pulleys and rigging spread over its surface. Lifeboats clung to its sides. Max looked around.

Still no sign of any life.

He hurried along the deck. He reached some glass double doors. He pulled them open and found himself on the ship's bridge. There was a central control console covered in hundreds of buttons and dials. It also had a computer workstation. There were also gaps where a couple more computers must have been. Wires were sticking out. Max stared at the loose wires. He thought back to the missing equipment at the research station. Was it the same thief who'd stolen from both the station and *The Triumphant*? And, if so, how did they get in? And what were they up to?

He left the bridge. He carried on walking, right over to the other side of the deck. He climbed down a twisting flight of steps. He reached a corridor and halted abruptly.

In front of him was what remained of a door. It had been smashed into thousands of fragments. They now lay scattered all over the floor. Max stepped through the splintered hole into the room. It was four times the size of the other cabins.

These must be Captain Hartnell's quarters. Or at least they were . . .

The place was a complete mess. Tables were overturned. Chairs were smashed to bits. Papers were strewn all over the floor. A cabinet had been pushed against the door as a barricade. This too lay in pieces.

Talk about utter devastation!

There were hundreds of oily marks all over the floor, mainly boot prints. But then Max noticed that some of these were much larger than the others. He placed his foot beside one. It was three times bigger than his own. Not only that, the large prints were footprints. And each foot seemed to have seven toes!

Was that what happened? Was the crew attacked by some kind of giant seven-toed beasts? Did they barricade themselves in here to try and fend off their attackers?

Max shivered.

Could any of the creatures still be on board?

He pulled out his digital camera. He took several shots of the giant footprints. There

didn't appear to be any further clues as to the identity of these attackers. He hurried back to the sailors' quarters. There he squeezed through the open porthole and eased himself down to the ground.

But the second his snow boots touched the ice, there was a great cracking sound. A circular sheet of ice flew up into the air. It left a large hole about ten meters away. Max gaped at the hole in astonishment. His heart was racing. He bent down to put on his snowshoes. Then a second circle of ice shot upward. It created another large hole, much nearer this time.

Max didn't hesitate. He started to run.

MAX FLASH
MISSION 5

CHAPTER 7

SMASH! Another hole was punched through the ice. This one was less than five meters away. CRASH! CRASH! Two more were smashed out, revealing the icy ocean below. Without snowshoes the surface was even more treacherous and slippery. Max had to work extra hard to stop himself from toppling over.

Max fled toward the place he'd left his backpack. *At least I know that's where I'll find solid ground.* As he ran, multiple holes exploded all around him.

He jumped, skidded, and swerved to avoid them. It was like running through sniper fire. He had seventy meters to cover before he made it back to shore. But then Max's right foot suddenly slipped. He fell, sliding straight toward one of the holes.

Nooooooooo!

He dug his left snow boot into the ice. He managed to stop a couple of centimeters shy of the hole. He struggled back to his feet and ran on. Ice sprayed all around him now. It crashed against his body and his head. He had thirty meters to go. A huge line of holes burst open just in front of him.

My route's being blocked!

His whole body was tense with determination. He ran onward, picking up speed. Then he launched himself into the most powerful long jump he could manage. His body arced through the air over the huge gap. He looked down into the icy water below.

If I fall in there I'm finished. I have to make it!

To his incredible relief, his feet smacked down on to solid ground. He turned back to look at the ocean. The sheet of ice between him and *The Triumphant* was pockmarked with holes.

He stood there, panting. Thoughts raced around his brain. *Someone or something wasn't too pleased about my investigations on board* The Triumphant. *Was it the creatures that attacked the crew? And who or what made all those holes in the ice?*

Max put on his backpack. For a moment all was silent and still. But this didn't last long. Suddenly, there was an ominous creaking sound. Max turned to see *The Triumphant* breaking free from its icy shackles.

The holes have broken the ice's grip on the ship!

With a terrible groan, *The Triumphant* began to plunge downwards. It disappeared below the waterline in thirty seconds.

I guess the navy's icebreaker won't be much use now.

Max stared out at the space where the ship had been. He thought back to the seven-toed footprints he'd seen in the captain's quarters. Maybe there'd be some more footprints in the snow. They might lead him to whatever it was that had attacked *The Triumphant*. He started following the shoreline to his right.

He studied the ground as he went. Unfortunately, the only thing he could see was snow. He stopped when he'd gone five hundred meters and returned to his starting point. He went left this time, but still no prints.

Max shook his head. With the temperature still dropping, he needed leads and fast. What had Zavonne said? *The temperature must NOT be allowed to reach −100 °C.* He began to tramp up the mountainside overlooking the coast. Not such an easy task without snowshoes. At last he reached the summit. He looked down at the valley he'd passed through earlier and pulled the snowboard out of his backpack.

Max placed the board on the ground and stepped onto it. He adjusted his foot bindings until he was comfortable. But then he spotted something in the snow. He crouched down to take a closer look.

Yes! A seven-toed footprint. And it looks pretty fresh.

Max glanced round. There was no sign of any life. He scooped up some snow from the footprint and emptied it into one of the plastic containers Jenkins had given him. He put the

container into one of his snowsuit pockets. He gazed into the valley.

There was another print and another. Max launched himself down the slope. He'd followed the trail about a hundred meters when he suddenly heard a faint rumbling. It was coming from somewhere high to his left. He glanced up. In the distance he could just make out two large white figures. They were far too big to be humans. But his gaze quickly shifted. A sheet of snow was hurtling down the valley in his direction.

No way! An avalanche!

MISSION 5

CHAPTER 8

Max was already too far down to climb back
up to the peak he'd just come from. And he'd
never be able to reach the other side of the
valley. He was trapped. The great mass of snow
was sweeping down toward him.

*How bad would that be? Escaping from
certain death in the frozen ocean only to be
buried by an avalanche!*

He shifted his weight to swerve to the right.
He leaned forward to up his speed.

I'm never going to make it!

Max began to feel the panic set in. But he suddenly remembered his gadgets. He reached behind him and grabbed the toggle of his Back-Fire Booster.

This better work!

The frontline of the avalanche was seconds away. It was descending at phenomenal speed. He pulled the toggle. Instantly, there was a loud popping noise and he was fired into the air. A split second later the avalanche flooded into the valley. It engulfed everything in its path. Max shot forward at incredible speed. He yelled with delight and relief as he flew above it.

After a hundred meters he dropped down onto a mountain ridge. The snowboard hit the ground. Max let it run for a few seconds. Then he swerved to a stop.

He watched in silence as the last of the snow crashed down into the valley. The entire path through the middle section of the valley was now completely buried.

Talk about a lucky escape!

Max studied the mountain ridges for the huge figures he'd seen earlier. But there was no sign of them. He had a strong feeling that these creatures were the same ones who'd attacked *The Triumphant*. He was also pretty sure that they'd had a hand, or paw, in starting the avalanche.

He had a final look around. Then he turned and headed back to the research station. He was eager to check out the snow sample he had collected. On returning, Max left his backpack, snow boots and snowboard in the

grey storage cube. Then he headed for the lab. He checked the thermometers: −59°C. Max frowned.

How on earth am I going to stop the temperature plummeting so fast when I don't know what's causing the drop?

There was no one around. He pulled the plastic container out of his pocket and emptied the snow sample onto a glass slide. He slipped this under a microscope on the workbench. He placed his eye to the viewing glass. He spotted it immediately—a long, coarse, white hair. It was far too long and thick for any human.

It must belong to one of the seven-toed creatures.

"What have you got there?"

Max was startled by Jenkins's voice. He looked

up as she walked across the lab.

"Er, it's just a bit of snow," he replied.

"So you managed to get some samples?" she asked. "Here, let me take a look."

"It's OK," Max replied, a little too quickly. "But thanks."

"No problem," she said with a slightly puzzled look.

Max scooped the snow sample back into the container. He slipped it into his pocket.

"I've got some data that compares the Bolt Zone with other regions of the Antarctic," said Jenkins. "I think you might find it useful."

Max groaned inwardly. He didn't have any time to look at data. But he couldn't keep turning down Jenkins's offers, or she'd get suspicious. So he spent the next half hour pretending to look at spreadsheets. But he kept an eye on the thermometers. They had dropped to –61°C.

"Thanks for that," said Max finally.

"Is there any chance I could check out the snowmobiles? I've never been on one before."

Snowboards were brilliant fun. But Max realized a snowmobile would be far quicker, especially for going uphill.

"Sure," said Jenkins. She reached over to a hook on the wall and pulled off a key. "This key'll work for all of them."

Max hurried down to the storeroom. He flicked a switch on the wall. A floor-to-ceiling steel shutter opened. Then he settled himself onto one of the snowmobiles. He turned the key. The engine roared to life. He twisted the handlebar throttle, and the machine leaped forward through the exit and onto the snow.

Superb!

He turned the handlebars and the snowmobile went to the left. He yanked the handlebars hard and skidded to his right. Max then increased his speed and spun the vehicle through a 180° turn.

This is awesome!

He turned round again. He was about to put the machine through another spin when a furious voice cut through the chilled air.

"WHAT ON EARTH DO YOU THINK YOU'RE DOING?!"

MAX FLASH MISSION 5

CHAPTER 9

It was Dr. Klosh.

He was standing in the storeroom entrance. He eyed Max angrily.

"THOSE VEHICLES ARE FOR RESEARCH TRIPS ONLY. THEY ARE NOT FOR PERFORMING MOVIE STUNTS!"

Max gulped and killed the engine.

"Sorry . . . I was just . . . "

"I'm sure he'll be using it for research," cut in a deep voice. "And anyway, I thought the 180° turn was worth watching!"

Max recognized the voice instantly. He spun round. There was Gruff Addison, all six foot four of him. He looked exactly as Max knew he would. Trademark chunky frame. Goatee beard. Piercing blue eyes. Beside him was an equally large guy with a full beard and a V-shaped dimple on his chin.

Saved by the earth's number-one survival expert!

Dr. Klosh frowned at Gruff's intervention. "All right," he muttered. "But no more fancy stuff, thank you." He turned and started climbing back up the ladder to the lab.

Max dismounted.

"Hi," said the TV star with a wide grin. "I'm Gruff Addison."

I know who you are!

"And this is my cameraman, Jim Sweeney."

"Howdy," said Jim with a nod of his head.

"You're the kid who's come out here to shadow Jenkins, right?" asked Gruff.

MAX FLASH

"Yeah, I'm Max. Thanks for stepping in."

"No worries," smiled Gruff. "Klosh can be a bit earnest."

Max laughed.

"Right," said Gruff. "Jim and I are going inside to check out the rushes we filmed this afternoon. Fancy taking a look?"

"Definitely," exclaimed Max. He tried not to sound *too* enthusiastic.

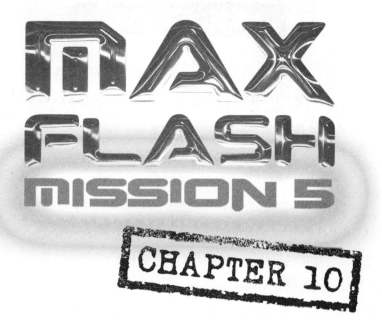

Max, Gruff, and Jim sat in the living room.
They watched some incredible footage on
a small playback monitor attached to Jim's
camera. Here was Gruff Addison leaping off a
sheer mountain face onto a sheet of ice. There
he was disappearing into a great mound of
snow. There he was again, skidding across the
bottom of a dangerously sloping crevice.

*This is unbelievable. I get to see the
unedited TV footage with the great dude
himself!*

Max had a million questions to ask Gruff. He was disappointed when Jenkins poked her head round the door to say that dinner was ready.

A short while later, Max was sitting at the dining table with Doctors Jenkins, Klosh, and Holroyd, plus Gruff and Jim. Klosh had obviously calmed down after his earlier outburst. There was no further mention of Max's antics on the snowmobile. Jenkins had prepared the supper. It was vegetable lasagna.

At first Max was taken aback by the speed at which everyone tucked into their food. But looking down at his plate he saw the reason why. His portion had come out of the oven piping hot. But it was already starting to freeze at the edges.

So that's what Jenkins meant when she said you had to be a quick eater here!

He'd taken a look at the thermometers before supper. They were touching −65°C.

It seemed to Max like it was almost that cold inside the station as well.

There was quiet for a while as everyone chewed. Max saw an opportunity to dig for info. "You know, this temperature-dropping situation," he began. He directed his comments at the scientists. "Are you still pursuing the theory that it's connected to freak windchill?"

"It's the *only* possibility," replied Holroyd. "But we're shocked by the *speed* at which it's dropping."

"I'm not sure windchill is the only explanation," said Jenkins thoughtfully. "I think there may be something else going on. It's kind of scary."

Max swallowed. *Has she discovered something weird out here, too?*

"Come on, guys. Let's not panic," cut in Gruff. "A temperature of −65°C isn't the end of the world. I was stranded at −85°C on an ice shelf once, for 48 hours. Sure, I nearly died. And it was weeks before any sensation returned to my fingers and toes. But I'm still here, aren't I?"

Max looked at the TV explorer with admiration. *This guy is awesome!*

After supper, Max helped Jenkins clear the table. When they'd finished, she spent some time playing with the heating system. It was situated in a cupboard in the corridor outside the bedrooms. Max watched as she used a screwdriver to twist a series of dials and pry some levers upwards.

"I've fixed it," she announced after about ten minutes. "It should at least last through the night."

"Nice one," nodded Max.

"I'm going to crash out," said Jenkins.

"Really?" asked Max. He glanced out of the window. It was still light, but when he looked at his watch it said 10:10 P.M.

Jenkins laughed. "You'll get used to it."

She went into her room. Max headed off to bed too.

I better get some sleep. I need to be fresh in the morning. I HAVE to get some leads tomorrow!

It was too cold to get undressed. He put on his thermal pajamas over his clothes. Then he dived into his microfiber sleeping bag. The day's exploits had left him totally exhausted. It wasn't long before sleep reeled him in.

CHAPTER 11

Max woke with a start. He checked his watch. The digits blinked 3:20 A.M. Out in the corridor he could hear a faint tapping sound. He turned over and tried to go back to sleep. But the tapping kept him awake. So he climbed out of his sleeping bag and stepped out into the corridor to investigate. Gruff was standing in front of the heating system cupboard. His back was to Max.

"Everything OK?" asked Max.

Gruff jolted with surprise and spun round.

"Oh, hi, Max," he said. "You startled me."

"Sorry," said Max. "What are you doing?"

"It's the heating. I know Jenkins fixed it earlier, but it's gone again."

"But she said it should at least last through the night," said Max.

"Did she?" said Gruff. "Well, it's obviously in a worse state than she thinks! I guess the tapping woke you, yeah?"

Max nodded.

"Well, I haven't been able to fix it this time. You get used to hardships when you're out here."

"I can imagine," said Max.

"There was this time I had to bury myself in an ice tunnel. It was during a mad snowstorm," laughed Gruff. "I must have been in there for at least twelve hours. Thought I might freeze to death. Kept my mind busy by thinking about the husky races I've competed in!"

The guy is more than a legend!

"I was impressed by the way you handled the snowmobile earlier," said Gruff. "And not everyone can cope with these conditions. It seems like you're doing pretty well. You could have a future in the TV survival industry!"

Me! Become like Gruff? Supreme!

"Anyway," said Gruff, "I'm off back to bed."

"Cool," said Max. He nodded good-bye and returned to his room. He climbed back into his sleeping bag. He slept well for the next few hours. He dreamed about being a top survival expert with his own TV show.

When he got up he found Jenkins in the kitchen preparing breakfast. "I can't believe the heating broke in the night," she complained.

"I know," agreed Max. "Gruff tried to fix it. But he had no luck. How about asking Klosh or Holroyd?"

"They're already out on a field trip," said Jenkins.

Just then Jim passed through the kitchen.

"Want some breakfast?" asked Max.

"Can't hang around," said Jim. "Gruff and I are off to film at a gorge. Gruff's going to do some free fall ice leaps!" Jim pulled a small vial out of his pocket. It had some sort of green liquid inside. He lifted it to his mouth. His face twisted as he drank it down.

"What's that?" asked Max. "Some kind of extreme-weather energy drink?"

"Yep, something like that," replied Jim. He was halfway through the door. "See you guys later."

Max prepared himself a bowl of cornflakes. He scarfed them down before the milk froze.

"Come and check out some snow level footage recorded by the cameras in the Viewing Dome," said Jenkins. Max had just finished eating. He sighed inwardly.

I desperately need to get out there and continue my investigations.

"Er, OK," he replied hesitantly.

The Viewing Dome was accessed via a ladder. It contained lots of different-sized telescopes. But Jenkins insisted they watch some prerecorded footage of snow levels in the vicinity. This was on the tedious side of ultra boring. Finally, Jenkins went to make some hot drinks. Max found himself alone.

He stepped over to the largest telescope. He stared through the glass. Outside, a wind had picked up. It was beginning to blow snow around. But then Max caught sight of two shapes through the snow. There, not more than a hundred meters from the station, were two huge beasts. They were at least seven feet tall. Their bodies were covered with thick coats of white fur. Their eyes were huge and crimson, and sunk back into deep eye sockets. Their teeth were as sharp as daggers. And they had seven toes.

Max sprinted down the ladder. He hot-footed it toward the lab. But as he went through the tunnel outside the kitchen he ran into Jenkins. He almost knocked the two piping-hot mugs out of her hands. "Where are you going?" she asked in confusion. "Nowhere," Max called back. "I just need to . . . get a bit of fresh air."

Max grabbed the snowmobile key from the lab. Then he dashed down to the storeroom. He picked up his rucksack and opened the steel shutters. He leaped onto the nearest vehicle and started up the engine.

The two snow beasts turned and started to run at the sound of the snowmobile.

They're frightened!

The creatures had a hundred-meter start, and they were running fast. But they'd be no match for a snowmobile.

The wind was howling. Snow swirled around him. Max hadn't got far when suddenly he heard a revving sound behind him. He glanced back. It was Jenkins! Her curiosity had obviously got the better of her. She was catching up fast on one of the other snowmobiles.

Disaster! She'll see the beasts and freak out. My cover will be blown!

It was an agonizing dilemma. Should he

turn back to stop her seeing the snow beasts? Or should he keep chasing them? It was too valuable a lead, so he sped on. He hoped he would lose Jenkins in the snowstorm.

Up ahead the beasts disappeared over a high ridge. A few seconds later Max's snowmobile flew over the ridge. It came smashing down on the other side with such force that he was thrown off. The vehicle skidded to a halt a short distance away. A dazed Max got to his feet. He was standing on a wide, icy plateau. There, not more than ten meters away, stood a group of *six* snow beasts. The group included the two who had led him there. But they didn't seem frightened any more. They looked menacing and dangerous. One of the beasts raised his fists in the air and let out a deep, earsplitting roar.

How could I have been so stupid? The snow beasts wanted me to follow them! It's an ambush!

CHAPTER 12

A second later, Jenkins came flying over the ridge. She too was thrown off her snowmobile. It crashed into Max's vehicle and came to a stop. She struggled to her feet.

"Run!" yelled Max. But it was too late. Jenkins had caught sight of the six snow beasts.

"W-w-what are they?" she asked in a quivering voice.

But Max had no time to explain. At that second the beasts pounced. Jenkins screamed

and stood frozen to the spot. Max acted instantly. He pulled out his Gum-Shooter Stun Gun and ripped off the top. At once the packet of gum transformed itself into a sleek weapon. He squeezed the trigger hard. Six bullets flew out. They sent the snow beasts flying backward.

Max headed for the snowmobiles. He pulled Jenkins with him. But the beasts were back on

their feet and beginning to advance again. He fired off another few rounds. He swept the gun through the air to scatter the bullets among the beasts. They were stunned and disoriented. This gave Max and Jenkins a valuable few seconds to reach their vehicles.

Max turned his ignition key and hit the throttle. The snowmobile roared to life and shot forward. When he'd gone ten meters he quickly glanced round to make sure Jenkins was following him. But she wasn't.

For some reason her machine hadn't powered up. And all six beasts were tearing toward her. Max spun around 180°. He pulled the trigger on the Shooter. Nothing. He'd used all twelve rounds!

There was only one thing for it. He pushed down on the

throttle and clung on like crazy as his snowmobile flew forward. Jenkins saw what he was doing. She leaped out of the way. The beasts didn't react as quickly. Max's machine plowed straight through them, sending them flying in different directions.

"GET ON!" yelled Max. He reached out a hand.

Jenkins grabbed his hand. She jumped onto the snowmobile. Max gritted his teeth as the vehicle shot forward.

"THEY'RE COMING AFTER US!" shouted Jenkins.

He looked back. The beasts were gaining on them. This would have been bad enough, but Max heard a sharp snapping sound and spied a crack opening in the ice up ahead. The ground was splitting in two! They needed to move fast. Otherwise they would be stranded on the wrong side of the crevasse. And they would be at the mercy of the snow beasts!

The gap was widening by the second.

"FASTER!" screamed Jenkins. She looked back in terror.

Max twisted the throttle as hard as he could. They accelerated toward the widening gap. He could hear the thundering of the beasts'

paws pounding behind him. The snowmobile was now going so fast that its front lifted off the ground. Max closed his eyes as it crashed through the air, with the deep crevasse below.

Please make it! Please make it!

The snowmobile began its downward trajectory. Max opened his right eye. To his immense relief, he saw that they were about to land on the other side.

"WE DID IT!" he yelled triumphantly. He turned back to look at Jenkins as the vehicle smashed onto the ground.

But to his horror, the seat behind him was empty.

CHAPTER 13

A mighty blizzard was now raging. Max could only just make out Jenkins on the other side of the crevasse. She was being dragged away by the snow beasts.

"NOOOOOOOOOOO!" Max screamed. He slammed on the brakes. The snowmobile twisted violently. He had to use every morsel of his strength to turn it round to face the crevasse. He hit the throttle. He was intent on flying back over the gap toward Jenkins and her captors. But the vehicle made a wheezing

sound. It refused to pick up enough speed to propel him over. It must have taken a bad hit on landing. And that must have affected its power. Max hit the handlebars in frustration and fury.

Zavonne's going to kill me. I've blown my cover. And I've got a scientist kidnapped by snow beasts!

Max drove along the edge of the crevasse as quickly as his snowmobile would allow. But there was no passing place between the two sides of the chasm. And he couldn't see any further sign of Jenkins.

He searched for two hours. It was an exhausted and very cold Max Flash who finally headed back to the station. The first things he saw when he walked into the lab were the thermometers. They were registering –84°C.

The temperature's heading towards –100°C fast. I still have to stop it getting there. And now I have to rescue Jenkins. Plus, I need to

find out what happened to the crew of The Triumphant.

Max went to the living room. He could contact the emergency services on the satellite communications equipment. He frantically tried to weigh the pros and the cons. On the one side, he badly needed help. But how seriously would they take him? His report would be that Jenkins had been kidnapped by seven-toed snow beasts. He entered the lab deep in thought. Just as he reached the satellite communications equipment, Gruff walked in.

"You look terrible," said Gruff. "What happened?"

Max stopped. He leaned against one of the work surfaces.

Maybe Gruff can help me. He knows this terrain better than anyone.

"It's Dr Jenkins," said Max quietly. "She's gone."

"Gone?" asked Gruff. "What do you mean gone?"

Max paused for a second.

Will Gruff believe me?

Max sighed deeply. "We were attacked," he replied. "By these . . . snow beasts. They dragged her away."

"Snow beasts?" Gruff raised his eyebrows. He looked over at the door to make sure no one was around. "I might be able to help you."

Max felt his spirits rise a little. "Really?"

"I've seen some strange things out in the snow,"

whispered Gruff. "Jim and I were once attacked by a giant ice lizard. You wouldn't find that in any wildlife book. And a cross between a polar bear and a lion once tried to eat me. There are some weird beasts out there. I don't go shouting about them because people would just think I was crazy. But some things can't just be explained away. You know what I mean?"

Max nodded. *What might Gruff know?*

"Anyway," Gruff continued, "we were out filming earlier today. And we found an entrance to some sort of ice cave. It didn't look natural. It was like someone had *built* it. And guess what? There were also some weird seven-toed footprints on the ground near the entrance."

Max stood bolt upright. An ice cave? Might Jenkins be there? And what about *The Triumphant*'s crew?

"So did you go in?" Max asked.

"We didn't have the right equipment on us," said Gruff. "But we're going back. Why don't you come with us? Maybe that's where Jenkins has been taken. And don't worry about being mauled by these beast things. I can handle anything out there."

Max frowned. "I'll definitely come with you. But I think we should contact emergency services first in case we need backup."

Gruff shook his head. "Let's say these weird beasts do have her. Then getting the emergency services to storm in might make things worse. After all, they've got no experience with things like that. They could put her in even *more* danger."

Max rubbed his eyes. He tried to figure out the right decision. "OK," he said, nodding. "We check out the cave now. But if Jenkins isn't there, we come straight back and contact the rescue services."

"Definitely," agreed Gruff. "Now let's go!"

MISSION 5

CHAPTER 14

A few minutes later, Max found himself down in the storeroom with Gruff and Jim. The blizzard had blown itself out. It was eerily quiet. Jim was stuffing film gear into a large backpack. Max and Gruff were refueling the three snowmobiles.

As they set out, Max scanned the landscape nervously. He expected some of the snow beasts to appear again. But his determination to rescue Jenkins kept his fear at bay. Plus, he had Gruff Addison in his party. Gruff could

handle anything. They drove over a mountain and then along the gorge where Gruff and Jim had been filming earlier. After about fifteen minutes, Gruff motioned to Jim and Max with a wave of his arm. They pulled over and got off their snowmobiles.

"It's just up ahead," said Gruff. He gave Max an encouraging look. "Don't worry. I bet we'll find her."

They tramped for about twenty meters. Then Gruff stopped. "Over here," he said. He pointed at an archway cut into the side of a cliff. Max studied it carefully. Gruff was right. It was too neat to have been formed naturally. Part of the entrance had already iced over in the extreme cold.

Max remembered the ice-melting solar panel he'd taken from the research station's roof. He reached for his backpack, but Gruff had already pulled out an ice pick. He smashed it against the surface. The ice splintered inwards.

"Come on," he said. He replaced the pick in his pack and stepped confidently through the gap.

Max and Jim followed close behind. The three of them found themselves in a short tunnel. It led to the top of an icy staircase. Above them were huge, spiked icicles. Sunlight poured through tiny holes in the roof. It gave the place an eerie blue glow.

"Wow!" gasped Max in amazement. "What is this place?" He turned to Gruff and Jim. Both of them looked equally awestruck.

"I have no idea," replied Gruff. "But we're going to find out."

They walked forward and stepped down the staircase. At the bottom were three tunnel openings.

Max took a deep breath. "Which one shall we take?" he asked.

Gruff was about to answer when a deep, bone-chilling howl filled the air. It was coming from the tunnel on the right and was followed by the sound of pounding feet.

Snow beasts!

"SPLIT UP!" commanded Gruff. He made for the tunnel on the right. "Jim take the one on the left. Max take the middle one!"

Max was about to question this strategy. (Was Gruff really going to take on the snow beasts alone?) But Gruff was the survival expert. Jim dived into the left tunnel and Max took the middle one.

The tunnel bent around a corner. Then it

dropped sharply.

Max lost his footing. He fell down onto his back and shot forward down the slope like a bullet.

MAX FLASH
MISSION 5

CHAPTER 15

Max crashed downward. He bounced off the hard icy walls for another hundred meters. Then he was spat out of the end of the tunnel into a passageway. There was no sign of the other two tunnels. There was no sign of Gruff and Jim. Up ahead was a tall archway. He crept forward and stuck his head a fraction around the opening.

He gasped at the sight before him. He was staring into a colossal circular chamber sculpted entirely from ice.

In the center of the chamber was a huge console. It was covered in flashing red buttons, dials, and silver switches.

Emerging from the top of the console was a wide glass chute, ten meters high. A gaseous cloud drifted up from the mouth of the chute. The cloud then drifted out through a large hole in the center of the chamber's ceiling.

Max looked to his right. He saw that around one semicircle of the chamber's walls were a series of large ice blocks standing in alcoves. A red tube spilled out from the bottom of each ice block. The tubes snaked across the chamber floor. They they disappeared into a panel on the base of the central console.

Within these blocks he could see dark shapes. But he couldn't make out what they were. Max quickly counted them. There were thirty. Twenty-nine contained shapes. One was empty.

Max looked to his left. He saw a selection of industrial thermometers. They were exactly like the ones at the research station.

So this is where the stolen equipment has got to.

Max gulped. The displays on the thermometers all read –94°C.

This must be where the temperature is being controlled from. But how is it happening exactly?

Max looked up. High above the floor of the chamber was a balcony. It circled the entire space. Perched on workstations were computer terminals. They were just like the ones onboard *The Triumphant*. There was no sign of any snow beasts. Max still felt his nerves jangling. He walked around the right side of the chamber. He reached the ice blocks. Max froze and gulped in horror.

Inside each ice block was a human!

MISSION 5

CHAPTER 16

At first Max thought all of the people were dead. But then he looked harder. Their bodies were absolutely still, but their eyes were moving from side to side. And then he saw a face he knew. It was Captain Edward Hartnell from *The Triumphant.* He recognized him from the distress signal Zavonne had shown him. Max's eyes scanned the row of ice blocks. He saw lots of men wearing naval uniforms—*The Triumpant*'s crew! The other trapped people were dressed in explorers' gear. And in the

twenty-ninth block was Dr. Stella Jenkins!

Max's brain was in overdrive. He struggled to figure out why these people were being kept prisoner inside ice blocks. *Are the snow beasts carrying out some sort of grotesque experiment?* But his thoughts were suddenly interrupted. He felt a tap on the shoulder. He jumped in terror. He spun round, expecting a snow beast attack.

It was Gruff.

Max let out a huge sigh of relief. "You were right," he whispered. "Jenkins is in here. And she's not the only prisoner. Let's get these people out. Then we can try and get to the bottom of this before the temp hits −100°C."

Gruff didn't move. And he didn't say anything.

"COME ON!" Max hissed urgently. "Let's get them out!"

Gruff remained motionless and silent.

"WHAT ARE YOU WAITING FOR?"

Gruff pulled a small vial out of his pocket. It contained the green liquid Max had seen Jim drinking earlier. He drank it in one gulp.

And then something weird started to happen. White fur began to spread over Gruff's face. This fur quickly covered his hands. And his hands were transforming into

paws with long curved claws. His whole body seemed to increase in size. Then his feet burst through his shoes. And his feet were hairy and seven-toed! His eyes sunk back into their sockets and went a deep shade of crimson with large black pupils.

"*No way!*" uttered Max in horror as he realized what was happening. He tried to pull away. But Gruff's paw shot out. He grabbed him in a viselike grip.

MAX FLASH
MISSION 5

CHAPTER 17

"GET OFF ME!" yelled Max. He struggled like mad as he stared in horror at the new Gruff.

"We've been keeping an eye on you from the second you visited *The Triumphant*," snarled Gruff. His voice was deep and guttural. His hot, salty breath flowed over Max's face. He pushed his face into Max's. His crimson eyes flashed with anger.

"So it was you who made those ice holes that nearly killed me!" said Max.

"Those under-ice explosives we took from

The Triumphant have their uses," growled Gruff. "But they obviously weren't enough to throw you off our trail."

"And the avalanche . . ." muttered Max.

"Again, you were lucky," hissed Gruff.

"What are you doing with all of these people?" demanded Max. Gruff's luminous eyes bored into him.

Gruff shoved Max forward until they were just a few meters away from the ice blocks. As they got nearer, Max got a much clearer view of the trapped humans. Their faces were

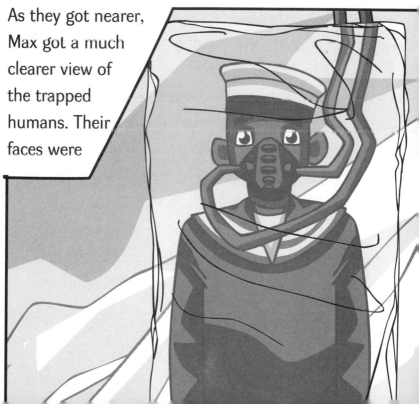

so pale they were almost transparent.

Each prisoner wore some kind of mask. The mask had a red and a blue tube running from it. Max noticed that the blue tube entered each ice block through its roof. Gruff followed his gaze and laughed. It was a harsh, grating cackle.

"Oh yes, we *do* feed them. Those blue tubes provide just enough nutrients to keep them alive. And their bodies are kept at just the right temperature not to kill them."

"Why are you keeping humans alive in blocks of ice?" yelled Max. He struggled again.

Gruff squeezed him tightly. "Well, our plan is so near to completion. I suppose there's no harm in telling you. We need their CO_2."

Max stared at the red tubes. They came out of the base of the ice blocks and led to the central console.

"To achieve our goal we need to collect CO_2 from humans," Gruff went on. "We combine

the gas they breathe out with a special concoction of chemical compounds in the console. When mixed together they produce *that!*"

Gruff pointed at the cloud of gas rising up from the console and out through the hole in the chamber's roof.

"I get it," said Max bitterly. "It's the gas that's lowering the temperature."

"Got it in one!" roared Gruff. "For our plan to be finalized, we need the temperature to fall to −100°C. Unfortunately we have a little problem. And that's where you come in."

Max looked at the thermometers stuck at −94°C. "Your console's broken down and you want me to fix it?" asked Max hopefully.

"The console is fine!" shouted Gruff. He revealed sharp yellow teeth. "And now it is time for the spectacle to begin."

Gruff clapped his hands. High up in the chamber at least a hundred snow beasts began to appear. Each took a place on the balcony. Each had a perfect view of the chamber floor.

"W-w-what are you doing?" asked Max nervously. A hundred pairs of hate-filled crimson eyes gazed down at him.

"MY FRIENDS!" roared Gruff, gazing up at the balcony. "THE TIME HAS FINALLY COME TO COMPLETE OUR PROJECT!"

There was an outbreak of cheering and whooping.

Gruff turned back to face Max. "The problem is that we haven't been able to collect quite enough CO_2."

I don't like where this is going.

"But we now have the last human we need to finish the job," said Gruff. He grinned hideously at Max. "YOU!"

MAX FLASH
MISSION 5
CHAPTER 18

Max gulped nervously. Gruff was now in full swing.

"You humans thought we were just a myth. You laughed at yetis, Bigfoot, and the rest of us. But we're as real as you!"

Gruff spat out the words.

"During the Ice Age *we* were the ones who inhabited the earth's surface. There was glorious snow and ice everywhere. It was delightfully freezing. We had thousands of miles in which we could roam. But the

earth warmed up. We were forced to retreat underground to small, icy chasms. Yes, it was cold enough down there for us to stay alive. But we were cramped and uncomfortable! You humans with your planet warming have kept us down there for thousands and thousands of years. Well, now it is time for the big freeze. When the temperature reaches −100°C the change will be irreversible. And it will be cold enough for us to return to the surface." Gruff looked up at the balcony. "Welcome to the NEW ICE AGE!"

There were thunderous claps and screams from the snow beasts. Max's mind whirred furiously.

Gruff wasn't fixing the heating system back at the research station. He was making sure it stayed broken to keep the indoor temperature as cold as possible for himself! And that's why he must have been at the station. He was in a perfect place to steal equipment. Plus the

snow beasts stole loads of equipment from The Triumphant—*not to mention the entire crew!*

"This new Ice Age will make the earth a home for us," shouted Gruff. "And for the yetis and Bigfoot and even Alfred—the one you humans call the Abominable Snowman."

Alfred?!

Max suddenly heard a loud clanking noise behind him. He twisted round and saw two snow beasts pushing a trolley. It held an ice block like the others. But this one was in two hollowed-out halves.

Max shuddered.

"Isn't it wonderful?" roared Gruff. He was playing to the gallery. "This stupid human boy thought he could stop us. But he'll end up being the one who gives us the extra CO_2 we need to complete the job! Why else does he think we led him here—for an iced tea party?"

There were screams of high-pitched laughter

from the balcony. Gruff clapped his paws. The laughter stopped immediately.

He lunged towards Max and lifted him clean off the ground. Max struggled and wriggled like crazy. But Gruff's grip was unbelievably strong.

"Say hello to your new home!" said Gruff. He gave Max a hideous grin. "We trust you'll be comfortable in there!"

"LET GO OF ME!" screamed Max. Gruff dropped him into one half of the ice block. Before Max could make a move, one of the snow beasts fastened a mask to his face. Gruff then heaved the other half of the block and dropped it onto the first. Max heard a loud click as the halves connected. The two parts of the ice block became one. The thirtieth prisoner was now firmly in place.

MAX FLASH
MISSION 5
CHAPTER 19

"NOOOOO!" yelled Max from inside his prison. The ice was so densely packed around him that he could hardly move. He cursed under his breath. Breath that was sending his CO_2 out through the tube and straight into the central console. Max watched in horror as the thermometers around the chamber suddenly dropped from $-94\,°C$ to $-95\,°C$.

Max's body shook with rage (in an extremely cramped fashion). *Gruff's right. It will be my CO_2 that's going to finish the job for them!*

He cursed himself for ever trusting Gruff. Gruff's cover as a TV survival expert had been absolutely brilliant. It hadn't just convinced Max. It had fooled millions of people the world over.

OK, I'm not going to stop them from inside this ice block. I have to get out. But how?

Max moved his lips a couple of centimeters forward. He took a sip from the blue tube. He sucked in a sugary liquid that tasted a bit like a flat fizzy drink.

Bearable, but not my future choice of beverage!

Max forced himself to relax his body as much as possible. He tried to lower his right arm. It moved a few millimeters, but no more. He was freeze-packed like a Christmas turkey! He tried his left arm. To his relief, there was a tiny bit more room on this side. He pressed his left arm against his body with all his might. Then he stretched it down as far as he could.

It was agonizingly slow. But his fingers finally reached his snowsuit pocket.

He looked out at the chamber. The thermometers had just reached −96°C.

I need to do this fast!

Max inched his hand inside the pocket. He curled his fingers around the Ice-Cutter Headphones. As he did this he remembered Zavonne's information.

If this ice is any thicker than fifty centimeters, the cutters won't work.

Out in the chamber, Gruff was flicking switches. He issued muffled instructions to the beasts up in the balcony.

Taking a deep breath, Max pushed his whole body back as hard as he could. This provided just about enough space in front of him for the next stage of his plan.

Max lifted the headphones up in front of him. He held them approximately thirty centimeters apart. He looked out of the ice block. His heart sank when he saw the thermometers move again, to −97°C.

He pushed the headphones against the ice block's surface. For a few seconds nothing happened. Just as despair was about to engulf Max, he heard a faint crackling sound. He saw a large circle appear in the ice. He could see that if he pushed the circle, it would topple forward. It would leave a big enough gap for him to squeeze through.

But Gruff was on the chamber floor. And a hundred other beasts were dotted around the balcony. As soon as Max escaped, they would be onto him in seconds.

He frantically tried to think of a way to distract Gruff and the snow beasts. The thermometers made a sickening movement: −98°C.

Max gulped.

Time was almost up.

MISSION 5

CHAPTER 20

*Never in the history of the world has anyone
needed a decoy as badly as I do at this
precise second.*

Max was in a state of desperation. Then
he suddenly had a brainwave. He pushed his
lips toward the dangling blue tube. Instead of
sucking, he *blew into it* as hard as he could.
A large red light on a steel wall panel on the
other side of the chamber began to flash. A
harsh alarm blared out. Max saw Gruff run
over to the panel. Max seized his chance.

He squashed his fists together. Then he
pushed the circle he'd made in the wall of the
ice block. There was a creaking sound. The
circle fell forward, thudding onto the chamber
floor. Max twisted his body. He pushed himself
out of the ice block and tore off his mask. All
eyes were fixed on the flashing panel. He had
almost reached the central console by the time
the snow beasts spotted him.

"THE BOY HAS ESCAPED!" hollered the
beasts from the balcony.

Max ran on toward the console. His heart
was pulsating wildly.

Gruff threw himself across the chamber
toward Max. Gruff reached out to seize Max's
ankles. But Max swerved out of the way and
launched himself through the air. He grabbed
hold of a steel lever on the surface of the
console and used it to begin his ascent up the
side.

"ATTACK HIM!" screeched Gruff. A split second

later,
Max
felt a sharp
pain in his
back. He looked
up. The beasts on
the balcony were pulling
icicles from the chamber
walls and hurling them at him.
One of these icy spears hit him
on the shoulder. He cried out in pain.
But he grabbed onto another lever on the
console. He pulled himself up further toward
the base of the glass chute.

More icicles flew down toward him. Max
lashed out with his feet to kick as many
off course as possible. But still one hit his
right arm. Another smashed against the
back of his legs, almost causing him to
lose his footing. He reached the base of

the chute just as the digits on the thermometers began to flash.

I'm never going to make it!

Icicles rained down on him. Max reached into his backpack. He pulled out the small solar panel. He threw it high into the air. His aim was spot on. The panel flew into the mouth of the chute. He heard it crash down against the sides of the chute and then come to a stop.

Immediately the shaft of sunlight shining down through the hole in the chamber's roof made contact with the solar panel. But when Max spun around to check the thermometers he groaned: −99°C. He'd done his best. But was it too late?

MISSION 5

CHAPTER 21

Max stared up at the chute, deciding his next move. A sudden gasp of shock came from every snow beast in the chamber. Max glanced at the thermometers again. They had stopped at −99°C. Max held his breath. Ten seconds later, the reading changed.

But this time *in the other direction.*

The thermometers returned to −98°C. Max's eyes widened.

"DESTROY HIM!" shrieked Gruff. A fresh wave of icicles smashed against Max. But he ignored the pain because the thermometers changed again. They went up to –97°C. And then, in quick succession, it went up to –96°C and –95°C.

Yessssssssssss! The solar panel is doing the trick! It's warming up the freezing concoction inside the console!

Max looked down. Gruff was standing by the console. He was frantically trying to open a hatch on its side to retrieve the solar panel. But however hard Gruff pulled, it wouldn't budge. The temperature continued to rise.

And then Max felt a couple of drips on his forehead. He looked up and saw that the chamber's icy roof was beginning to melt. Still the temperature rose. The drips started falling faster. It wasn't long before they'd turned into drops. Max leaped down from the console and landed on the chamber floor.

Console dealt with. Now it's time to free the prisoners.

The temperature hit −55°C. Max heard groans coming from the beasts on the balconies.

The temperature is getting too warm for them!

A couple of chunks of the chamber wall became dislodged and fell down. Max sidestepped them and ran across to the ice blocks. He'd almost reached them when he heard the beasts' groans become tortured howls. He looked back. Several beasts were leaping down from the balcony, then lying on the chamber floor in an attempt to keep themselves as cold as possible.

Max skidded to avoid a falling beast. He ran to Jenkins's ice-block prison. He pushed at its top half a couple of times, but it didn't budge. So he shoulder barged the block and smashed the top clean off.

He helped a freezing and terrified Jenkins to climb out.

"You need to get the others out of here as fast as possible," he instructed Jenkins.

"B-b-but y-y-you a-a-are . . ." she stuttered, still shivering.

"Forget about me," commanded Max. "There's a small opening in the chamber wall over there. It's right where the ice is melting."

And even though Jenkins could only shuffle slowly, she made it to the next ice block. She helped Captain Hartnell kick open a hole through the slushy surface. Then together they started freeing the others.

Max turned back to face the center of the chamber. A huge opening had appeared in the floor. Snow beasts were rapidly flinging themselves into it.

That must lead back down to the icy chasms Gruff spoke about!

The thermometers now read −40°C. Max felt a streak of satisfaction. But this was short-lived. He suddenly felt a powerful hand

wrap itself around his throat.

"NOW YOU'LL SEE WHAT A REAL PRISON FEELS LIKE!" screamed Gruff.

CHAPTER 22

Gruff gripped Max firmly and dragged him toward the opening. Huge chunks of ice were now smashing down onto the chamber floor. The rest of the beasts were diving into the ice chasms. And as the hole widened further, the central console dropped out of sight, too.

"You may have wrecked our plan," barked Gruff. "But you're going down with us!"

Max shuddered. He imagined what it would be like in the freezing chasms deep below the earth. He realized he only had a few seconds

to save himself. He suddenly reached out, grabbed a handful of fur on Gruff's chest, and pulled it as hard as he could.

"Aaaarrrgggghhhhhh!" screeched Gruff. Gruff let go of Max and twisted in pain. Max leaned forward and shoved Gruff on the back. Gruff toppled over into the hole. Max heard Gruff cry, "YOU HAVEN'T HEARD THE LAST OF THIS!" as he fell.

Torrents of water were now gushing down.
Max ran toward the hole through which
Jenkins and Captain Hartnell had led the
other prisoners. But Max's path was suddenly
blocked. Towering over him was a snow beast.
Its dark crimson eyes scorched with venom.
Max spotted something in his hand—
a video camera. It was Jim!

"Gruff may have failed, but I won't!" he
roared. He puffed out his chest and reached for
Max. Max ducked. Jim swiped the air, dropping
his camera to the ground.

Max didn't waste a second. He grabbed the
camera and whacked it against Jim's back. It
flew out of his hands and skidded after Jim,
across the chamber floor and down into the
huge hole. Max dived out of the way as a
massive chunk of ice crashed to the ground.

Time for a quick exit!

But the way out was now blocked by the
chunk of ice.

Max sprinted toward the wall of ice. He kicked out as hard as he could. He knocked out a small opening and dived through. He hit the ground outside, picked himself up, and started running. A split second later the entire ceiling collapsed, along with the chamber walls.

Max turned around. He stared at the giant mound of snow and melting ice. If he hadn't been inside the chamber, he wouldn't have believed it had ever existed. He turned around again. He saw a group of freezing and exhausted people up ahead. He ran over to them and located Jenkins.

"W-w-who . . . are you?" she mouthed through chattering lips.

Max was mindful of the need to keep his identity secret. He replied, "No one." Then he leaped onto one of the snowmobiles and sped back to the research station. As soon as he was inside, he grabbed the satellite communications equipment. He contacted emergency services. His call was picked up instantly. He issued his instructions. "We need as many helicopters and personnel as you can spare. We are at the following coordinates in the Bolt Zone . . ."

CHAPTER 23

Three hours later, Max went to say goodbye to
Dr. Klosh and Dr. Holroyd.

"Bye, guys, thanks for all your help," said Max.

The scientists nodded. "The temperature
now seems to have stabilized," said Klosh,
turning to Holroyd.

Oh well, what did I expect?

Max made his way out. The DFEA helicopter
was waiting. It hovered above the ground. He
climbed up the ladder. The pilot gave him a
thumbs-up, and they sped off.

At the airport, Max waited for his flight home.
He was waiting in the departure lounge. A news
bulletin on a screen caught his attention.

"News has come in of a major search and
rescue operation. The focus is an area of the
Antarctic known as the Bolt Zone," announced
the newsreader.

Max's eyes lit up.

"We're hearing that among those rescued
were the captain and crew of the stricken
British navy vessel *The Triumphant—*"

The newsreader pulled an incredulous face.

"I've just been handed an update. It states
that a number of explorers who vanished in
the region were also among the survivors.
Some were reported missing as far back as two
years ago. They were exceptionally cold. But
remarkably, none of them were suffering from
hypothermia. The survivors have been relaying
all kinds of stories. Many are talking about
being frozen in ice blocks by strange Yeti-like

creatures. One of them, a Dr. Stella Jenkins, spoke of how a remarkable boy managed to free everyone. On the line we have Dr. Tarquin Carruthers. He is a psychology specialist in extreme-weather survivors. Dr. Carruthers, what do you make of these statements?"

"People who suffer long periods stuck in the snow often speak in a nonsensical fashion when they're freed. I call this post-ice babble."

"What about these reports of a mystery boy?"

"This 'boy' is no more than a figment of their imaginations. He's a symbol of their freedom. It will be interesting to hear what the survivors have to say once their bodies and minds have returned to their usual temperatures."

The newsreader moved on to another report. Max turned away from the screen.

Hmm, I managed to free everyone. And I stopped the temperature from reaching −100°C. But have I blown my cover?

CHAPTER 24

On touchdown, a taxi was waiting for Max.
It wasn't long before he was home. His mom
gave him an almighty hug when he came in
through the front door.

"We saw the reports on the news," she said.
"We're incredibly proud of you."

"M-o-m," said Max, extricating himself from
her grasp.

"She's right," beamed his dad. He squeezed
Max's shoulder affectionately. "It sounds like
you did a first-class job out there."

"I did my best," replied Max.

"Zavonne wants you down in the communications center for an immediate debrief," said Mom.

Max was in no hurry to see Zavonne. By the time he made his way down there, her face was already on the large plasma screen.

I just hope I'm not in too much trouble!

"I'm not very happy about you damaging one of the snowmobiles," was Zavonne's opening comment.

I don't like where this is going . . .

"Luckily for you, though, Dr Jenkins has been told you left the region well before her 'escape'. She is now fully convinced she was hallucinating down in the ice chamber. She's also sure that her capture by the snow beasts was invented by her traumatized mind."

Thank goodness for that.

"I take it that Doctors Holroyd and Klosh don't suspect your involvement in any of this?"

"They're too wrapped up in their research," replied Max.

"Am I right in understanding that the snow beasts' infrastructure was totally destroyed? And that all of them returned to their ice chasms? And that the temperature in the Bolt Zone has returned to normal?"

Max nodded.

"Well, that's something," noted Zavonne through pursed lips.

A thought struck Max. "Er, Zavonne?"

"Yes?"

"You know my Californian holiday was cut short. And I missed out on all of that sun and surfing. Well, does the DFEA have any sort of compensation package? You know—something to make up for my lost watersports time?"

Zavonne thought about this for a few seconds.

At last, I'm going to get something decent out of her!

A metal drawer on the wall started flashing.

"Look inside," instructed Zavonne.

Max pulled the drawer open expectantly. He picked out a small rectangle of card with writing on one side:

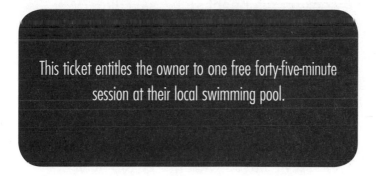

This ticket entitles the owner to one free forty-five-minute session at their local swimming pool.

Zavonne's face vanished from the screen. Max groaned.

Unbelievable!

He tramped up the stairs. Half of him was furious with Zavonne for her ingratitude. But the other half was already waiting for her next summons. For Max Flash, the next mission couldn't come soon enough.

EPILOGUE

Miles beneath the earth's surface, a large crowd of snow beasts sat squashed together in a freezing, cramped, and dimly lit ice chasm.

"Look on the bright side," said Jim. "We *nearly* made it. If that kid had been a minute later with the solar panel stunt, we'd have been sipping snow cocktails from ice glasses now."

"*Nearly* isn't good enough!" snapped Gruff. "I should've stayed with my TV job. It beats being stuck down here."

"Hang on a second," said Jim. "My camera fell down with me. We can still make films. What do you say?"

"Films about what?" griped Gruff. "The darkness and boredom we're going to experience over the next million years?"

"That's a starting point," Jim said with a grin. He grabbed his camera.

Gruff sighed wearily. "OK, I'll do it."

"Just smooth down your fur on top a bit," instructed Jim.

Gruff patted his fur. "Better?" he asked.

Jim gave him a thumbs-up and pressed the standby button.

Gruff cleared his throat. He pulled his most winning TV smile.

"And action!" called Jim.